The Chip Woman's Fortune
by Willis Richardson

Introduction
by Vanessa Cross

AF897648

9 8 7 6 5 4 3 2 1

The Chip Woman's Fortune can be performed royalty free.

ISBN: 9781795287630 (Paperback)

Library of Congress Cataloging in Publication Data:
Richardson, Willis, 1889-1977
[Plays. Theater. African-Americans.]

The Chip Woman's Fortune (1923)

A play by Willis Richardson

Willis Richardson was not the first African American to write a play, but he was the first one to have a play produced on Broadway. He is noted as the most prolific writer of his generation, with six of his plays produced. A highly respected playwright, his plays were performed in high schools and colleges, as well as by theater companies across the United States. Several of his 46 plays were published in various magazines. As a drama anthologist, he edited three anthologies of plays by African-Americans.

Before the the Black Power movement of the 1960s, Richardson was focusing in on Black history heroes such as Crispus Attucks, the first person to die in the Boston Massacre (*Attucks, the Martyr*), and Antonio Maceo, a central leader in the Cuban rebellion against Spain (*Antonio Maceo*). Alexandre Dumas, the French-born playwright and novelist of African descent also found voice in Richardson's plays (*The Elder Dumas*), as did African royalty such as Massinissa, the founder of the Kingdom of Numidia (*Near Calvary*), as well as Emperor Menelik II of Abyssinia (Ethiopia) (*In Menelik's Court*).

Often considered father of African-American drama, Richardson believed history was best learned when dramatized. This is why he gave many of his plays a historical base. Most of his plays were also drawn from a folk tradition that honed in and examined central conflicts within the Black community. He believed that African-American playwrights should not focus on racial tensions, in what he believed was catering to the interest of White audiences. In his essays, Richardson opined that African-American playwrights should instead focus on the internal conflicts within the Black community.

In 1922, Willis Richardson wrote the one-act play *The Chip Woman's Fortune*. On January 29, 1923, it was performed by the Ethiopian Art Players under Raymond O'Neil in Chicago. It moved on to community theaters in Washington, D.C. and New York. On May 7, 1923, the play had a short run at the Lafayette Theater in Harlem, which has the distinction of becoming the first major theater in the United States to desegregate in 1913. On May 15, 1923, *The Chip Woman's Fortune* became the first African-American drama to reach Broadway when it opened at the Frazee Theater.

The "Chip Woman" is Aunt Nancy, a kindly old woman. We find her living with Silas Green as a caregiver for his ill wife, Liza, whom we learn is making a steady recovery under Aunt Nancy's watchful care that is added by her vast knowledge of natural roots. Aunt Nancy also contributes to the household by picking up chips of wood and lumps of coal from the streets.

Silas learns that the family's greatest treasure – a Victrola – is about to be repossessed due to a financial strain that has left him temporarily furloughed and unable to make payments on the outstanding debt owed on the record player. After discovering that Aunt Nancy has managed to save some money from street donations she receives, Silas decides that it is time for her to contribute more than the nursing care provided to his wife, and the wood chips and coal lumps she collects for use by the family. Aunt Nancy, however, has other plans for her savings.

– Vanessa Cross (2019)

CHARACTERS

Silas Green, a store porter

Liza, his wife

Emma, their daughter

Aunt Nancy, the Chip Woman

Jim, her son

Two other men

ACT I

The scene is the very plain dining room of a poor colored family. The floor is without covering, and the walls are without pictures. At the center of the floor is a rectangular table with a couple of chairs near it. In the rear wall is a fireplace in which a low fire is burning, and at the left of this sits Liza in a rocker. She is wrapped from the shoulders to ankles in blankets, for she is just up from a spell of sickness. At the right of the fireplace is a window. A door at the right leads through to other rooms and to the back yard. Another door at the left leads to the front of the house. Against the left side near the door stands a Victrola. There is a deep silence as Liza sits gazing into the fire. She looks up at the clock on the mantel, then looks towards the right and calls:

LIZA: (*calling*) Emma! Emma!

(*Presently Aunt Nancy appears at the right. Every one of us has seen her king—those old women who go about the streets picking up chips of wood and lumps of coal, or searching in trash cans for whatever they can find. Such is Aunt Nancy. She is old, and her back is bent on account of constant stooping. She is wearing a bonnet which partly hides her black, wrinkled face, and is wearing a shawl over her shoulders.*)

AUNT NANCY: You callin' Emma, Miss Liza?

LIZA: Yes'm, Aunt Nancy. You seen her?

AUNT NANCY: No'm, Ah ain't seen her?

LIZA: Wonder where she is? Ah want her to go to the store for me.

AUNT NANCY: Ah don't know where she is. Ah ain't seen her for the last two hours, but I reckon she'll drop in in a minute or two. How you feelin now?

LIZA: Ah'm feelin' pretty good. The medicine you give me last night must be doin' me good.

AUNT NANCY: Ah don't reckon you need no more medicine today.

LIZA: Ah reckon not. How you feelin'? Seems like Ah ought to be askin' you that instead of you askin' me.

AUNT NANCY: Ah'm feelin' right sharp for a old woman. To tell you the truth, Ah ain't felt better since the day Ah got married. Ah'm 'spectin' somethin'.

LIZA: You 'spectin' somethin'?

AUNT NANCY: Yes'm.

LIZA: What you 'spectin'?

AUNT NANCY: Ah can't tell you that, Miss Liza; but maybe you'll find out before the day's gone.

LIZA: Is it anythin' good?

AUNT NANCY: Didn' Ah tell you Ah ain't felt better since the day I got married?

LIZA: Ah'm glad somethin' good's happenin' to somebody. Ain't nothin' good happenin' to me.

AUNT NANCY: You getting' better, ain't you?

LIZA: Yes'm. Ah'm getting' better.

AUNT NANCY: (*going close to her*) Lemme look in your eyes.

(*after looking into her eyes*) Your eyes is startin' to shine. You'll be getting' all right pretty soon. (*She whispers something into Liza's ear.*)

LIZA: (*blushing*) Oh, no'm. Aunt Nancy!

AUNT NANCY: (*laughing*) That's all right, you wait. Ah likes to see a woman's eyes shinin'. It shows she's got some life in her. Ah don't like to see no woman with dead eyes, 'specially a young woman. Ah likes to see 'em pert.

LIZA: You ain't by yourself. Everybody likes to see a young woman pert.

AUNT NANCY: Ah was goin' in the woods to dig up some roots, but Ah reckon Ah'll wait 'til tomorrow.

LIZA: Tomorrow'll be all right. You don't have to go today.

AUNT NANCY: Ah'll go now and set out on the back steps and think. Ah like to set in the sun and think.

LIZA: Think about what?

AUNT NANCY: Ah got somethin' to think about.

LIZA: What?

AUNT NANCY: Ah can't tell you everythin'. It ain't goo to tell everythin' you think about, you know. 'Spose everybody told all their thoughts?

LIZA: That wouldn't never do.

AUNT NANCY: 'Deed it wouldn't never do. Everythin' ud be upside down with other people knowin' what you was thinkin' about. (*She starts out right.*)

LIZA: If you see Emma out there send her in to me.

AUNT NANCY: All right, Ah will. (*She looks through the right door.*) Here comes Emma now.

(*Emma enters. She is a pretty brown girl of eighteen.*)

EMMA You want me, Ma?

LIZA: Yes, Ah want you. Where you been?

EMMA: Upstairs.

LIZA: Upstairs doin' what?

EMMA: Combin' ma hair.

LIZA: Combin' your hair this time o' day? You combed your hair once this mornin'. What you comb it again for?

EMMA: Ah wanted it combed.

LIZA: You wasn't always so fond o' combin' your hair. What's comin' off?

EMMA: Nothin'

LIZA: (*looking at her more closely*) Come here, gal. (*Emma moves nearer to her.*) Ah believe before God you been puttin' powder on your face. Is you been puttin' powder on your face? (*Emma looks away without answering.*) Where'd you get that powder from?

EMMA: Ah bought it.

LIZA: Bought it with what? (*as Emma is silent*) Don't you hear me talkin' to you? Bought it with what?

EMMA: Bought it with some change Pa gave me.

LIZA: Well, wipe it off! Wipe it right off and don't put no more on! Leave it up there and Ah'll use it when Ah get on ma feet. You too young to be powderin'.

AUNT NANCY: (*who still stands near*) Let the gal alone, Liza. You was young like that once and she ain't goin' to be that young but once.

LIZA: She don't have to paint herself up like a billboard just because she's young. (*to Emma*) Get the basket. Ah want you to go to the store for me.

(*Emma goes out right.*)

AUNT NANCY: Ah'll be out on the back steps if you want me.

LIZA: All right'm. Ah hope Ah won't need you.

(*Aunt Nancy goes out right, and Liza sits rocking until Emma returns. She speaks just as Emma comes in.*)

LIZA: There's somethin' mighty funny goin' on round here. You primpin' and Aunt Nancy thinkin'. Ah reckon we goin' to have a thunder storm.

EMMA: Ain't nothin' funny goin' on.

LIZA: What you doin' plasterin' your face up and comin' your hair if somethin' funny ain't goin' on? You know you ain't never combed your hair twice the same day in your life it it wasn't Sunday.

EMMA: (*anxious to change the subject*) What did you say to get from the store?

LIZA: Get some potatoes and chops and some cakes. Some o' the little ones your Pa likes so much.

EMMA: Is that all?

LIZA: Yes, that's all. Look a here, tell me this. Did Aunt Nancy take you in the woods and show you how to dig them roots yesterday?

EMMA: Yes'm, she showed me, but Ah don't remember much.

LIZA: Why don't you? You ain't got your mind on no body, is you?

EMMA: No'm She says she's goin' to show me all over again so Ah'll know how to find 'em for you when she's gone.

LIZA: Aunt Nancy ain't goin' nowhere.

EMMA: Ah hope she won't, but if she does Ah'll be sorry. She's so good to me. Ah love her a lot.

LIZA: 'Deed she is good. Everybody loves her and they can't help it. Ain't no way in the world to help lovin' somebody that's good to you.

EMMA: And Aunt Nancy sure has been good to us.

LIZA: Nobody knows that like Ah do.

EMMA: (*starting out*) Ah'm goin' now.

LIZA: Wait a minute. Start the Victrola off before you go, and go out the back way, it's nearer.

EMMA: (*adjusting the needle*) When we goin' to get some new records, Ma?

LIZA: New records? You better wait 'til the Victrola gets paid for. You got a plenty o' records.

EMMA: But they'll all old.

LIZA: That's all right, you can keep on usin' 'em. You ought to be glad to get bread to eat and let new records alone.

(*Emma starts the machine and goes out right.*)

LIZA: Don't stay long.

EMMA: (*outside the door*) No'm, Ah'll be right back.

(*Liza is listening to the Victrola when Silas, her husband, enters from the left. He is a man about forty and is wearing the uniform of a store porter. As he enters Liza looks up at him in surprise.*)

LIZA: Why, Silas, what you doin' home?

SILAS: (*throwing his cap down and moving to the table*) They sent me home.

LIZA: No discharged?

SILAS: (*no in the best of spirits*) No, Ah ain't discharged, but it's almost as bad; Ah'm furloughed a couple o' days without pay.

LIZA: Furloughed for what?

SILAS: (*motioning towards the Victrola*) On account o' that old Victrola. Seems like it's bringin' us more trouble than it's worth.

LIZA: What's the Victrola got to do with your job?

SILAS: It's just like everything else. When a man's got trouble o' one kind seems like everything goes wrong.

LIZA: That ain't tellin' me nothin'.

SILAS: Well, you know we ain't paid nothin' on that Victrola since the first payment, don't you?

LIZA: Yes, Ah know that. But you been promisin'.

SILAS: That's the trouble. Ah been doin' a lot o' promisin' and no payin'.

LIZA: (*impatiently*) Well, what else? You just as well tell me all of it at once. Ah don't feel like askin' a million questions.

SILAS: The man said he was goin' to send here and get the thing if we didn't pay this month, didn't he?

LIZA: Yes.

SILAS: Well, you know we ain't been able to pay, so he's goin' to send after it.

LIZA: Goin' to take it away?

SILAS: Yes.

LIZA: So, that's why you got furloughed, is it? 'Cause they goin' to take the Victrola away.

SILAS: No, that ain't it exactly.

LIZA: Ah see you ain't told me. What is it exactly?

SILAS: The manager o' that music place is a friend o' ma boss; and this mornin' while Ah was sweepin' off the front pavement he passed by me goin' in the store. When he seen me he stopped and looked at me hard, then he went in. Ah thought trouble was comin' when Ah seen him look at me so hard. After he came out the boss called me in and told me they was goin' to send after that Victrola; and then he says, "Go home and stay a few days and maybe you'll learn how to pay your debts." So here Ah am.

LIZA: Ah'll be mighty sorry to lose that Victrola; but if it can't be helped, it can't be helped.

SILAS: No, it can't be helped, but that ain't the worst of it. If Ah don't pay and they take it back, when Ah go back the boss'll always have his eyes on me, and Ah bet it won't be long before Ah'll be losin' ma job.

LIZA: What you goin' to do?

SILAS: Ah'll do anything to save ma job.

LIZA: Ah know you'd like to pay and keep the Victrola; vut Ah don't see where you goin' to get the fifty dollars from.

SILAS: Ah know one thing.

LIZA: What?

SILAS: Aunt Nancy's got to start payin' for her room and board.

LIZA: (*surprised*) Aunt Nancy!

SILAS: Yes. We can't keep her around here as high as everything is.

LIZA: (*earnestly*) But look what she done for me. She brought me from flat o' ma back. Ah had one foot in the grave before she come here. And look at me now. Ah'm almost on ma feet.

SILAS: Ah can't help it. Ah know she done a whole lot for us, but Ah can't keep things goin' if she don't pay.

LIZA: She helps along. She picks up chips and pieces o' coal on the street. That keeps you from havin' to buy 'em.

SILAS: Everythin' you sayin' is true, but she's either got to give us some money for stayin' here or she's got to go.

LIZA: (*greatly concerned*) If she goes who's goin' to nurse me? Who's goin' in the woods to get the roots to make my medicine?

SILAS: If that old woman's didn't have money, Ah wouldn't say nothin'.

LIZA: (*not understanding*) If she didn't have what?

SILAS: If she didn't have money; but Ah know she's got money.

LIZA: (*angrily*) Where in the devil would Aunt Nancy get any money from?

SILAS: Ain't no use to get made about it. Ah know what Ah'm sayin'.

LIZA: How do you know she's got money?

SILAS: Ah know because Ah been watchin' her the last week or so.

LIZA: You been watchin' her, is you? Well, what did you find out?

SILAS: Ah found out that people passin' in the street give her money every day.

LIZA: You ain't talkin' about a cent or two anybody might give a poor old woman, is you?

SILAS: No, every day Ah see people givin' her dimes and nickles and quarters. And it ain't no longer than yesterday that Ah seen two rich lookin' men giving' her greenbacks.

LIZA: Ah ain't never seen her with no money.

SILAS: Ah know you ain't. She hides it.

LIZA: Hides it where?

SILAS: In the back yard. I know the very place.

LIZA: Did you see her hide it there?

SILAS: No, Ah didn't see her hide it there, but every time I go out there by that spot she come right up.

LIZA: Why didn't you wait 'til she went away?

SILAS: I done that twice; but every time Ah went out there she come right back just like somethin' drawed her back. Once Ah went out there with a spade and up she comes and stands right on the spot. Ah told her Ah wanted to dig a hole for a post and she said, "Please don't dig it right here, Mr. Silas; Ah got somethin' planted here." You know if somebody has anything planted, they wouldn't go and stand right on the spot.

LIZA: (*after a moment's thought*) Well, whether she's got money or not, Ah don't think you ought to put her out after what she's done for us.

SILAS: That's the only way I know we can get by.

LIZA: That won't make it the right thing to do. A lot o' people get by by doin' the wrong thing. Ah know Emma won't like it.

SILAS: It's got to happen just the same is she don't hand out some money. Where's Emma?

LIZA: She went after somethin' for dinner.

SILAS: When she comes in, tell her what Ah said. 'Course the old woman might get open-hearted and let us have fifty dollars or so; then we won't have no trouble at all and Ah can go back to work tomorrow.

LIZA: Maybe she'll let us have that much if she's got it, but Ah don't believe she's got that much.

SILAS: (*determined*) Somethin's got to be done. (*as he starts out*) Ah reckon Ah better change these clothes so they'll be clean when Ah do go back.

(*He goes out leaving Liza gazing into the fire. Presently, Emma returns with the basket on her arm.*)

LIZA: Ah got a lot o' sad news for you, Emma.

EMMA: (*a little frightened at her mother's tone, rests the basket on the table and gazes at her*) What's the matter? Anythin' bad happened?

LIZA: They goin' to take the Victrola away.

EMMA: The Victrola! Who's goin' to take it away?

LIZA: The men from the store's comin' 'cause we ain't been making no payments.

EMMA: Does Pa know about it?

LIZA: Yes, he's the one told me.

EMMA: He been here?

LIZA: He's here now. They sent him home from work because we ain't been makin' no payments.

EMMA: (*fearfully*) He ain't been discharged, is he?

LIZA: He ain't been discharged, but he's furloughed and that's just as bad.

EMMA: You mean they goin' to let him go back?

LIZA: Yes, they'd let him go back today if he could make a good payment on that Victrola; but he reckons he'll have to stay out two or three days as it is.

EMMA: Ah'm mighty sorry they put him off, and Ah'm mighty sorry we can't keep that Victrola. Hearin' that thing was about the only pleasure ah had.

LIZA: That ain't the worst yet.

EMMA: What, somethin' more? What else is it?

LIZA: You Pa says if Aunt Nancy don't pay some money for stayin' here she's got to go.

EMMA: Where's Aunt Nancy goin' to get any money from?

LIZA: He says he's been seein' people give her money almost every day, and she's got it buried in the back yard.

EMMA: If she's got any money at all, it's just a few cents; but Ah don't believe she's got none.

SILAS: (*Entering just in time to hear what Emma says. He is now wearing overalls.*) Yes, she is got money, too; and she'll either have to pay some or get out.

EMMA: (*turning on him*) Ah don't see nothin' fair in that. She picks up chips, she brings home wood and coal, and she nurses Ma. What more do you want?

SILAS: (*sitting at the right of the table*) If she'll give me a few dollars or let me borrow a few dollars, maybe Ah can go back to ma job tomorrow.

EMMA: If you put her out, Ah believe Ma'll go right back to bed cause there won't be nobody that'll know what to do for her. So Ah don't see nothin' you'll gain by puttin her out.

SILAS: If she'll let us have the money –

EMMA: If she's got any money it's just a little she's savin' for her son.

SILAS: (*surprised*) Her son! Ah didn't know she had no son.

EMMA: Yes, she, she's got a son.

SILAS: Where's he? Ah ain't heard nothin' about him.

EMMA: He's been in the pen a long time, but Ah reckon he's out now.

SILAS: In the pen?

EMMA: Yes, seh.

SILAS: (*still puzzled*) And she's savin' money for him?

EMMA: Ah reckon that's what she's savin' it for if she's got any.

SILAS: (*in disgust*) Well, for God's sake! Savin' money for a jailbird!

EMMA: She says she wants him to have a few cents to keep him 'til he can get a job.

SILAS: Did she tell you all this?

EMMA: Yes, she. Ah wrote a letter for her the other day.

SILAS: (*turning to Liza*) Did you know anything about this, Liza?

LIZA: No, this is the first time Ah've heard a word about it.

SILAS: Why didn't you say somethin' about it?

EMMA: You always told me to tend to ma own business. Ah didn't want to be tellin' her business around.

SILAS: It's all right to tend to your own business, but it ain't all right to keep secrets from your parents when it concerns 'em. You say her son's out now.

EMMA: He was to be out yesterday. She's lookin' for him to come here today.

SILAS: What was he sent up for?

EMMA: Ah don't know, seh; somethin' about a woman, Ah believe.

SILAS: And he means to come here, does he?

EMMA: Yes, seh.

SILAS: You hear that, Liza?

LIZA: Yes, and Ah ain't particular about havin' no jailbird comin' here neither.

SILAS: Ah reckon Ah just as well talk to her now as any other time. Was she out there when you come in, Emma?

EMMA: Yes, seh, she was sittin' out on the back [steps]; but she got up when Ah came in and started off.

SILAS: Well, go tell her to come in here a minute.

EMMA: (*as she goes out*) Ah'll have to catch her 'cause Ah reckon she's gone.

SILAS: Just go out there and stand by that middle clothes prop and she'll come right in sight. Ah've already tried it a lot o' times myself.

(*Emma goes out.*)

SILAS: Liza, Ah want you to understand Ah'm not acting' this way 'cause Ah mean to be hardhearted. Ah've just got to get out o' this trouble.

LIZA: (*discouraged*) Ah'm sorry everything turned out like this, cause I reckon Ah'll have to go back to bed if she goes.

SILAS: (*concerned*) Don't say that. The Lord couldn't be that hard on us.

LIZA: Ah hope you're right; goodness knows Ah do.

SILAS: If Ah can get her to do us this favor before the men come after that Victrola, everything'll be all right. (*There is a pause while they ponder over the situation*). And even if she will agree to help us, Ah'm tired o' this kind of' life. Ah'm sick o' livin' from hand to mouth.

LIZA: Ah reckon we ought to be thankful to be livin' any kind o' way with all the trouble we had. Some people get along better'n we do, but a whole lot o' others don't get along as good. Ah only got one consolidation besides believin' in the Lord.

SILAS: What's that?

LIZA: That things ain't always been like this, and they might not always be like this.

SILAS: Ah hope not. (*after he listens*) Here they come.

LIZA: Now don't be hard on her, Silas. You know she's been mighty good to us.

SILAS: I ain't goin' to be hard on her. Ah'm goin' to be as fair as Ah can.

(*Emma enters followed by Aunt Nancy.*)

AUNT NANCY: (*moving to the table and speaking to Silas*) You want to see me, seh?

SILAS: (*kindly*) Yes'm, Aunt Nancy, Ah want to talk to you. Get a chair so she can sit down, Emma.

(*Aunt Nancy looks around for a chair; Emma brings her one and she sits above the table.*)

SILAS: The first thing Ah want to do, Aunt Nancy, is to thank you for all the good things you done for us. And then Ah want to tell you that we're in trouble.

AUNT NANCY: You all in trouble, Mister Silas?

SILAS: Yes'm. The men'll be here today after the Victrola, and Ah'm put off from work a few days 'cause Ah didn't pay for it.

AUNT NANCY: Ah'm might sorry for that.

SILAS: And you know you been stayin' here with us for six months or more and we ain't been chargin' you a thing.

AUNT NANCY: No, and Ah wouldn't a been able to pay you nothin' no how.

SILAS: Now Ah'm askin' if you'll pay us for stayin' or let us borrow a few dollars from you?

AUNT NANCY: (*with a long face*) 'Deed the Lord knows Ah can't pay you nothin', Mister Silas. Ah ain't got nothin' for myself.

SILAS: But we know you got money hid out there in the back yard.

AUNT NANCY: Ah got a little money out there, but that ain't for me; that's for ma child.

SILAS: (*feigning surprise*) You didn't tell us you had no child.

AUNT NANCY: Ah reckon you'd call him a man, but Ah call him ma child. He's grown.

SILAS: Where is he?

AUNT NANCY: Ah reckon he's on his way here now.

SILAS: (*still pretending ignorance*) Ah don't see what a old woman like you wants to be savin' money for a grown man for. He ought to be workin' and takin' care o' you. Ain't he workin'?

AUNT NANCY: He's been locked up.

SILAS: In jail?

AUNT NANCY: In the pen.

SILAS: That's so much the worse. You oughtn't to be savin' money to give to a jailbird.

AUNT NANCY: (*offended*) He ain't no jailbird, Mister Silas; don't call him that. He's ma son.

SILAS: He ought to be shamed of hisself for not workin' and takin' care o' you.

AUNT NANCY: That used to be the way when Ah was comin' up. When children used to get grown they used to take care o' the old folks, but now it's different. The old folks has to take care o' the children.

SILAS: Ah wouldn't never look out for no grown man.

AUNT NANCY: Ah reckon you wouldn't Fathers wasn't never like mothers and never will be.

SILAS: And 'specially if he went to the pen.

AUNT NANCY: Goin' to the pen ain't nothin'. Some o' the best men in the world's been to the pen. It tain't the goin' to the pen that counts, it's what you go there for. Once it used to be a big disgrace to be locked up; but the people in them days forgot that the Lord was locked up. No, seh, it ain't the bein' locked up, it's what you locked up for. If the Lord had a got locked up for stealin' something' or killin' somebody do you think people would be praisin' him like they do?

SILAS: I know they wouldn't; but what did your son get locked up for?

AUNT NANCY: He got locked up about a woman, but he done what any other man might a done. He was goin' with a woman what he thought was clean, but she was crooked. He run up on her one night when another man was handlin' her kind o' rough and beat the man up—he beat the man up bad. Then he found out the woman was crooked and he lost his head and beat her up too. That's the worse part of it.

SILAS: (*doubtfully*) And they sent him to the pen for that? Just for that?

AUNT NANCY: Yes, seh. The man he beat up was one o' these big fellows what went to church every Sunday, and looked so clean and nice in his biled shirts and white collars and fine clothes all through the week days, but in the night he trailed in the gutter. He used his pull and put up a job on Jim that sent him to the pen.

SILAS: Ah don't mean to hurt your feelin's, Aunt Nancy, but your boy can't be much if he beat a woman up.

LIZA: 'Deed he can't.

AUNT NANCY: (*hanging her head*) That's the worse part of it. Ah didn't mind him beatin' the man, but Ah never did care much for a man that ud hit a woman—no man but ma own son. (*looking him in the eyes*) And you know a mother can't help that.

SILAS: Ah always did think some mothers was too kindhearted.

AUNT NANCY: No, they ain't. Mothers ain't half as kindhearted as God is. If God was hard as some people is, everybody in this world would be farin' mighty bad. You know there ain't no man perfect, and no woman neither.

SILAS: I reckon you might be right about that, but the main reason I sent for you was to ask you if you wouldn't let us have a little money. If you can't do it we'll be in a hole sure enough.

AUNT NANCY: Ah wish Ah could. Ah'd be willin' to do anything in the world for you, but he comes first, you know.

SILAS: Do you reckon he'll let us have it?

AUNT NANCY: Ah don't know; he's mighty kindhearted. He's takin' a mighty long time to come here too.

(*At this time, there is a loud knocking on the outside door.*)

AUNT NANCY: (*starting to rise*) Ah reckon that's him now.

LIZA: Don't get up, Aunt Nancy; Emma'll let him in.

(*Emma goes out.*)

SILAS: (*to Aunt Nancy*) Why don't you take your bonnet off? You don't want to look like you ain't home.

AUNT NANCY: Never mind. Ah'll keep it on. We won't be here long, Ah reckon.

EMMA: (*returning*) It's the men after the Victrola.

(*Silas hastens out left.*)

AUNT NANCY: (*sighing*) Oh, Lord, Ah thought that was Jim. Ah wonder why he don't come?

LIZA: Don't worry, Aunt Nancy, it ain't late.

EMMA: Ah reckon he might be lookin' for the place.

AUNT NANCY: But you put this number in the letter, didn't you?

EMMA: Yes'm, Ah put it in.

SILAS: (*returning*) Ah don't know why Ah done it, but Ah told 'em to wait a few minutes.

(*He sits again.*)

AUNT NANCY: Ah don't know. Jim might come in a few minutes.

(*There is another knock on the door.*)

SILAS: (*rising*) Ah wonder what they want now?

(*He goes out again.*)

AUNT NANCY: That might be Jim.

LIZA: Ah hope it is.

(*Silas returns followed by Jim. When Aunt Nancy sees him she flies towards him. Jim opens his arms and draws her to him.*)

AUNT NANCY: (*holding him off and looking at him*) It is you, sure enough? Jim, is it you?

JIM: (*smiling*) Yes'm, it's me.

AUNT NANCY: Come over here.

(*She draws him over to the table and we have an opportunity to get a good view of him. He is about thirty, standing over six feet in height and large in proportion. He is wearing a blue shirt with collar attached and a blue suit.*)

AUNT NANCY: These is the people Ah been stayin' with all the winter, Jim. (*She names each one in her way of introduction.*) This is Mr. Silas.

JIM: (*smiling as they shake hands*) Glad to meet you, Mr. Silas.

AUNT NANCY: This is Miss Liza.

JIM: (*bowing to Liza*) Glad to meet you Miss Liza.

AUNT NANCY: And this is Emma. (*Jim and Emma bow and smile at each other*). These people been mighty good to me, Jim.

JIM: (*speaking to all of them*) Ah'm glad to hear that and Ah thank you all for it.

LIZA: We ain't been half as good to her as she's been to us.

EMMA: Indeed we ain't.

AUNT NANCY: Ah ain't done nothin' that no good woman wouldn't a done. Jim knows me.

JIM: Ah know her well, too.

AUNT NANCY: (*to Jim*) What made you take so long to get here?

JIM: Well, Ah hung around a little while—

AUNT NANCY: Now, Jim, you ain't got no business hangin' 'round when Ah'm waitin' for you.

JIM: And even when Ah got here Ah wasn't sure this was the right place 'cause Ah seen tow men hangin' round on the outside and they looked kinder like bootleggers.

SILAS: Them's the men that come to take the Victrola away.

JIM: (*turning to Aunt Nancy*) You say these people been good to you, May?

AUNT NANCY: Yes, they been mighty good to me.

JIM: (*reaching into his pocket*) Ah got fifteen dollars. You can have that if it'll do you any good. (*He gives it to Silas.*)

SILAS: (*taking the money*) Thanks for that. Maybe some o' these days—

(*The two men who have been waiting outside enter.*)

FIRST MAN: Ah'm sorry, but we can't wait all day; we got to get back to the store.

JIM: (*to Silas*) How much do you owe on it?

SILAS: Fifty dollars.

JIM: Fifteen dollars won't do much good then, will it?

SILAS: Well, it'll help. Ah been tryin' to borrow it from your Ma.

SECOND MAN: (*roughly*) Come on, Dan, let's take it; they ain't got nothin'.

SILAS: (*as they take hold of the Victrola*) Wait a minute!

JIM: (*turning to his mother*) You got any money, Ma?

AUNT NANCY: Ah got a little Ah been savin' for you.

JIM: How much?

AUNT NANCY: (*who is not very good at figures*) Ah don't know, but ah reckon it's enough. Ah'll get it. (*She goes out right.*)

SECOND MAN: (*impatiently*) Come on, Dan; this is all a bluff.

(*They move the Victrola towards the door*)

JIM: (*getting in the doorway*) There ain't nobody or nothin' goin' out o' here 'til she comes back!

(*Jim is such a large man and so nearly fills the doorway that the two men stop and reconsider their plan. They decide to wait.*)

JIM: Ah don't mean no harm to nobody and Ah wouldn't hurt a hair in nobody's head; but when Ah say wait, Ah mean wait.

FIRST MAN: But you see, mister, we been waitin' a long time already.

JIM: Well, you won't have to wait much longer. She'll be back in a minute.

(*Aunt Nancy returns with a rather dirty box which she puts on the table and opens. All gaze into it.*)

AUNT NANCY: (*pouring the contents of the box on the table*)

This is yours, Jim. Ah been savin' it for you ever since you went away.

JIM: (*staring at the money*) All this for me?

AUNT NANCY: Yes, and you can do anything you want to do with it.

JIM: (*pushing half of the money to Silas*). Here, take this; maybe it'll be enough.

(*Judging from the expression on Aunt Nancy's face Jim is giving away too much.*)

SILAS: (*drawing the money to him*) 'Deed it will be enough. (*After counting the money he hands part of it to one of the men.*) Here's your fifty dollars.

(*The first man takes the money and with the aid of the second man pushes the Victrola back to its place. Having done this they start out.*)

JIM: (*to Silas*) You better get a receipt for that.

SILAS: (*to the men*) Hey, wait a minute. (*The men stop.*) Gimme a receipt for that money. (*The first man writes him a receipt and then they go out.*) That's better. (*after indicating the money left on the table*) Ah reckon you better take the rest of it back, Jim.

JIM: No, you keep it. You all been good to Ma, and ain't nothin' Ah got too good for you.

LIZA: She done a whole lot more for us than we could ever do for her.

AUNT NANCY: Ah'd a give you that money before, Mr. Silas, but Ah was savin' it for Jim, and Ah just didn't have the heart to give it away.

SILAS: That's all right, Auntie; Ah 'preciated it just as much as if you had give it to me when Ah first ask you.

AUNT NANCY: (*taking up her basket*) Well, Jim, Ah reckon we better be goin'.

LIZA: (*quickly, in surprise*) Goin'! Where you going'?

AUNT NANCY: Goin' to get a place to stay.

JIM: Then Ah'm goin' to look for a job.

LIZA: But Ah thought you was goin' to stay here with us.

AUNT NANCY: You ain't got no room for both of us, chile.

SILAS: (*shifting the chairs around*) Yes'm, we is. We'll make room.

JIM: No, seh. Ah don't want you to cramp yourself on ma account. It won't take us long to find another place.

LIZA: But how'll Ah get along, Aunt Nancy, with you gone?

AUNT NANCY: Ah won't be far away. Ah'll come in and look after you every day.

LIZA: Ah'm mighty sorry you goin'; and Ah want to thank you for what you done for us.

AUNT NANCY: (*as she and Jim stand near the door*) Maybe we'll ask you all to do us a favor sometime.

SILAS: And we'll be mighty glad to do it.

AUNT NANCY: Well, good day 'til tomorrow.

SILAS, LIZA & EMMA: Good day.

JIM: Good day to all of you.

SILAS, LIZA & EMMA: Good day.

(*Aunt Nancy and Jim go out.*)

EMMA: Ah'm sorry she's gone.

LIZA: You might be mighty sorry he's gone too by the way you look at him.

SILAS: Deed she must be. She looked at him like her life depended on it.

LIZA: To tell the truth, Ah'm mighty sorry she's gone too. She's sure goin' to be a loss to me.

SILAS: But she says she's goin' to come around every day to look after you.

LIZA: Yes, but that ain't like stayin here.

SILAS: Well, there ain't nothin' Ah can do.

EMMA: Ah reckon you're mighty glad you didn't put her out.

SILAS: Ah am, Ah'm mighty glad.

LIZA: She got us out o' trouble, all right.

EMMA: Indeed she did.

SILAS: Ah got to go and get ma work clothes on and go and see about ma job.

LIZA: She saved your job too, Ah'm thinkin'.

SILAS: You bet your life she did.

(Curtain)

Made in the USA
Monee, IL
18 October 2026

66035055R00021